Bob's Boots
and Other Stories

One morning Bob walked into his front room carrying a big box.

"Look, Finn!" he said excitedly. "The postman has just delivered this. I wonder what's inside?"
Finn pressed his nose up against his glass tank and watched Bob open the box.

"My new boots have arrived!" cried Bob, holding them up for Finn to see. "What do you think of them?" he asked.

The goldfish did a back-flip. **Splash!** He really liked Bob's new boots!

"I think I'll wear my new boots to work," said Bob.

When he walked out into the yard, Wendy was giving the machines their jobs for the day.

"Lofty, you're with Bob today," she said. "Muck and Scoop, you're with me."

"Morning, Wendy," called Bob.

"Morning, Bob," Wendy replied.

Bob walked around the yard proudly.

"What do you think of my new boots?" he asked them.

"They're very smart," replied Wendy.

Bob stopped and looked around.
   "Can anyone hear squeaking?" he asked.
   "I can't hear anything,"
said Lofty.
   Bob started to walk again
and the squeaking came back.
Squeak, squeak, squeak!
   "I can hear it now," said Wendy.
   "Hee, hee!" giggled Dizzy.
"It sounds like mice."
   Lofty started to shake all over. "Ooohhh!
Don't say that, Dizzy. I'm scared of mice!"

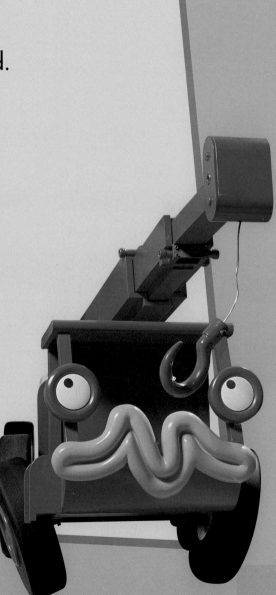

As Bob walked towards Wendy, the squeaking got louder and louder.

"Ah ha! I think I know where it's coming from," said Wendy.

"Where?" asked Bob.

"You sound like you need oiling, Bob!" chuckled Scoop.

"Your boots!" laughed Wendy. "They need wearing in, to soften up the leather."

"I think I'll walk to the job today," said Bob. "I need to wear my new boots in!"

"Come on, Lofty!" he said, and waved goodbye to the others as they set off in the opposite direction.

Lofty clattered slowly along with Bob walking behind him, carrying his lunch box.

Squeak, squeak, squeak!

Further up the lane, Bird was listening to Travis and Spud, who were trying to work out the quickest way to Bob's yard.

"You go left at the crossroads," said Spud.

"I'm sure it's right..." muttered Travis.

"No, no, no!" cried Spud.

Just then, Farmer Pickles came past, so they asked him to settle the argument.

"They say the quickest way is usually as the crow flies," he replied.

"It means the quickest way to get anywhere is to go in a straight line."

"Come on, Travis," said Farmer Pickles, "We've got work to do."

When they had gone, Spud turned to Bird and boasted, "I can run faster than any old bird can fly! I'll race you to Bob's yard!"

"Toot, toot!" cried Bird as he flew off.

In a nearby field, Lofty was trying to lift a heavy gate, but the strong wind was making it a bit tricky. "Careful now," said Bob as he helped lower it into place.

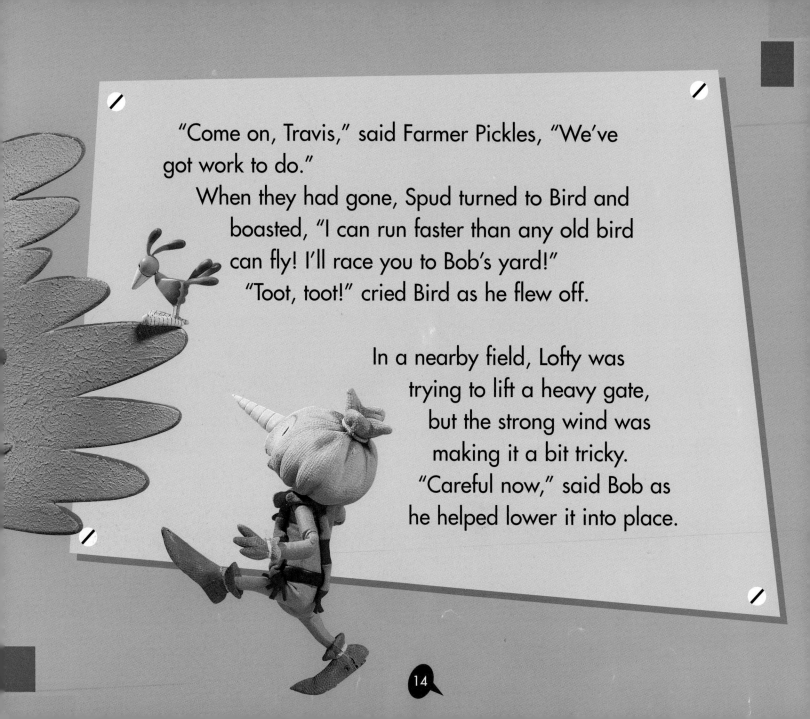

"Phew! Time for lunch!" said Bob as he opened his lunch box.

"Oooh, what have you got today, Bob?" Lofty asked.

"My favourites! Cheese and chutney sandwiches and a big cream bun," Bob replied.

Suddenly a gust of wind blew the paper napkin from the top of Bob's sandwiches.

"Whooah!" cried Bob as he chased after it.

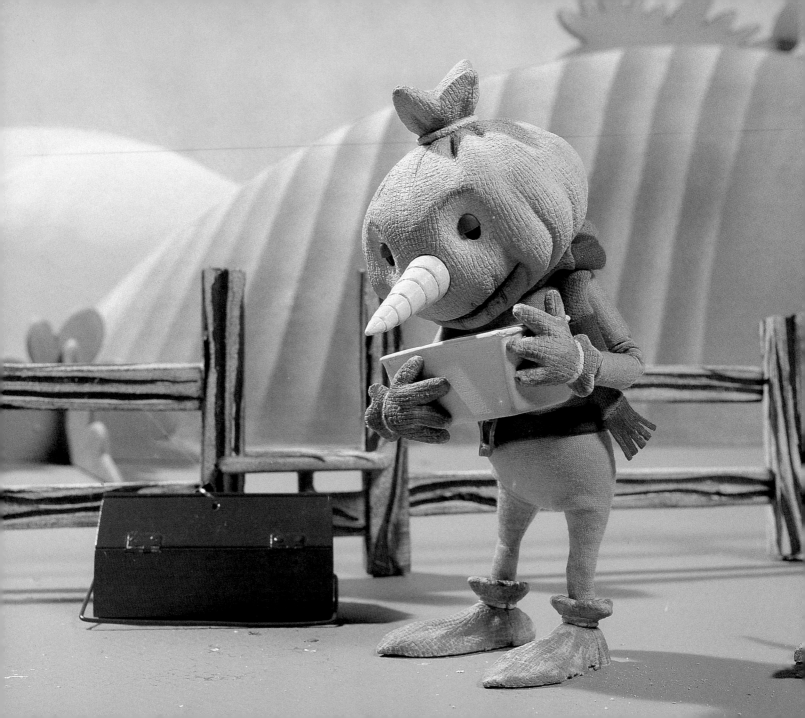

Meanwhile, Spud and Bird were racing across the countryside. Spud stopped when he noticed Bob's lunch box with the sandwiches and big cream bun inside.

"Mmmmm!" he said as he nibbled the sandwich. He was just about to take a big bite of the cream bun when he spotted Bird flying away.

"I'd better save this bun until I get to Bob's yard," he said, racing off after Bird.

In the next field, Bob was still chasing after the paper napkin.

Squeak, squeak, squeak!

Three little mice heard the noise and thought it might be a friend! They jumped up and followed the sound of Bob's boots.

Finally, Bob managed to catch the napkin and went back to his lunch box, followed by the mice. When he got back he couldn't believe his eyes.

"Hey! Who's been eating my sandwiches?" he cried. "and my cream bun's gone! Have you seen it, Lofty?"

Lofty was just about to say he hadn't seen the sandwiches, when he spotted the three little mice peeping out from behind Bob's new boots.

"Aaaargghh!" he shrieked as he darted down the road. "M… m… m… mice!"

"Mice?" said Bob. "Where?" But the little mice had scurried around behind Bob's back.

Bob chased after Lofty and the mice chased after Bob's squeaky boots!

"Come back, Lofty!" cried Bob.

Squeak, squeak, squeak!

Wendy, Muck and Scoop were filling a skip with rubbish from an old kitchen, when Bird zipped overhead, followed by Spud.

"Hello, Wendy!" called Spud. "Can't stop! Bye!"

"What is going on?" puzzled Wendy.

Back at the yard Roley was snoozing and Dizzy was playing, when suddenly Lofty came roaring in.

"Umm, what's the matter, Lofty?" rumbled Roley sleepily.

"M…m…mice!" stammered Lofty. "They're chasing me!"

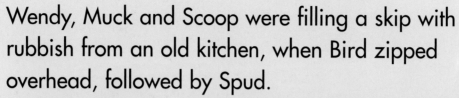

24

Bob rushed into the yard after Lofty.

"Lofty, there aren't any mice. Look!" said Bob,
turning around. But this time the mice stayed still
and he spotted them.

"Oooh," said Bob. "Lofty, you were right!"
The three little brown mice looked up at Bob.

Bob walked round in a circle and the mice followed him.

"Ha, ha! Look! They like my squeaky boots, don't they?"

"I don't like mice though," quivered Lofty.

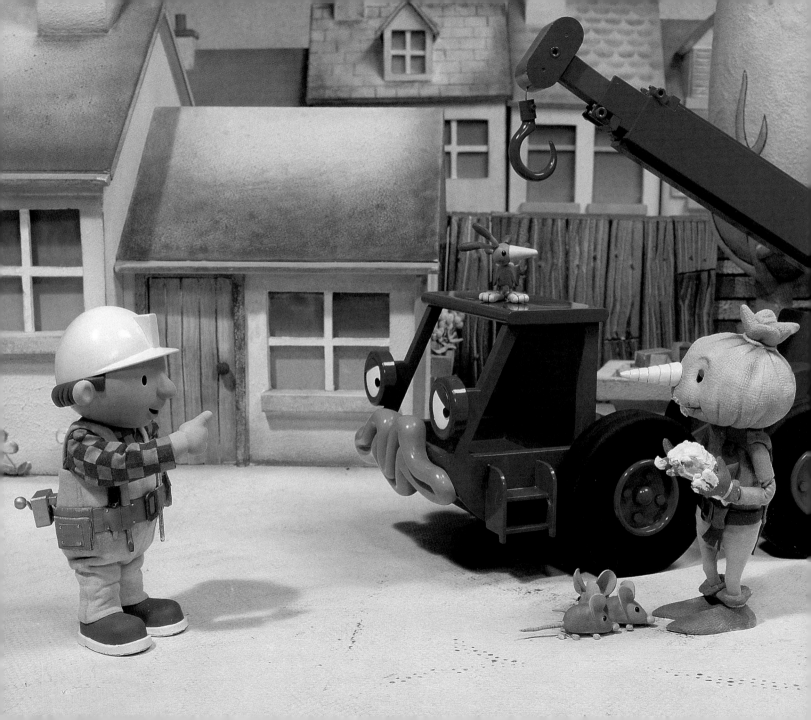

Just then, Bird came whizzing into the yard and landed on Lofty.

Spud dashed in a moment later, gasping for breath.

"I've beaten Bird!" he cried.

"Toot, toot!" whistled Bird proudly.

"Oh, no," grumbled Spud as he spotted Bird. "But at least I can eat my cream bun."

"That's my bun, isn't it?" Bob asked sternly. "You know you shouldn't take other people's things without asking."

"Sorry, Bob," mumbled Spud. Feeling embarrassed, he stared at the ground where he saw the three hungry mice looking up at him.

"Go away!" he shouted.

As Wendy, Muck and Scoop turned into the yard, they saw Spud running down the road with the three mice scampering after him.

"Leave me alone!" Spud yelled.

"**Squeak, squeak, squeak!**" went the mice as they followed him down the road.

"Hello, Wendy!" Bob called, as he walked towards her.

"Bob! Your boots have stopped squeaking," said Wendy.

"I must have worn them in with all the running about I've been doing," Bob chuckled.

"Have you had a busy day?" Wendy asked.

"Not really," Bob replied. "You could say it's been as quiet as a mouse!"

THE END!

Dizzy's Mix-up

Bob was having an early morning cup of tea before he started work.

"Miaow!" cried Pilchard, who wanted to play.

"Sorry, Pilchard. I've got lots to do. I'll play later," Bob promised.

Wendy and all the machines were waiting for Bob in the yard.

"Today we're going to put bollards around the town hall," Bob told them.

Dizzy looked puzzled. "Ooh, what are bollards?"

"They're things you stick in the ground to stop the traffic," Bob explained.

"Mrs Potts is having some garden statues delivered," Wendy told Bob. "She was hoping you could dig a few holes before they arrived."

"A few holes shouldn't take too long," said Bob.

"Thanks, Bob," said Wendy. "Mrs Potts will be very relieved."

Bob loaded the road drill into Muck's front scoop, then put edging stones into Scoop's shovel.

"What can I take, Bob?" squeaked Dizzy.

"How about a big bag of cement?" chuckled Bob.

They were soon all loaded up and ready to go.

"See you later," rumbled Roley.

"Yeah… er, bye!" said Lofty, a little nervously.

"**Can we dig it?**" called Bob as they clattered out of the yard.

"**Yes we can!**" cried Muck, Scoop and Dizzy.

When they arrived at the town hall Bob showed Dizzy and Muck where to start work. Then he set off on Scoop to Mrs Potts' house.

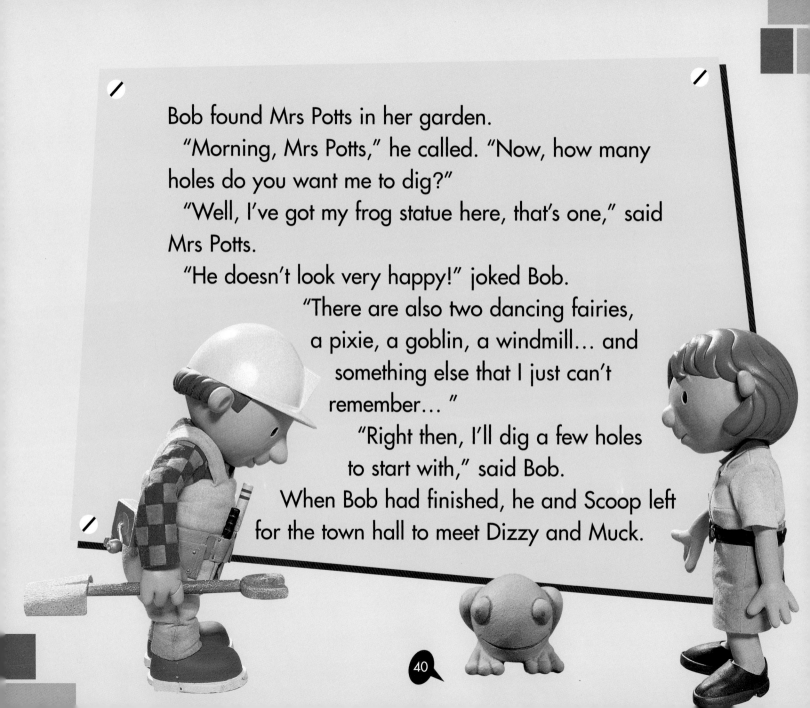

Bob found Mrs Potts in her garden.

"Morning, Mrs Potts," he called. "Now, how many holes do you want me to dig?"

"Well, I've got my frog statue here, that's one," said Mrs Potts.

"He doesn't look very happy!" joked Bob.

"There are also two dancing fairies, a pixie, a goblin, a windmill... and something else that I just can't remember... "

"Right then, I'll dig a few holes to start with," said Bob.

When Bob had finished, he and Scoop left for the town hall to meet Dizzy and Muck.

First, Bob drew a line of chalk crosses on the road in front of the town hall. Then he lifted the heavy road drill out of Muck's front scoop.

"Cover your ears!" he yelled to the machines, as he put on his ear protectors and safety goggles. "This is going to be really **LOUD!**"

Bob switched on the drill and held on tight. It screeched and started to shatter the hard concrete. Vibrations from the powerful drill made Dizzy bounce wildly up and down!

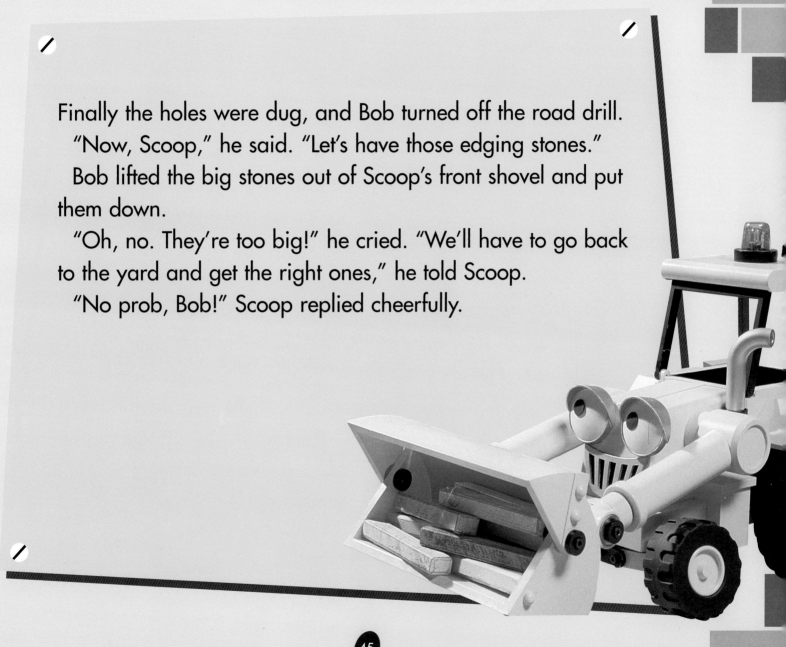

Finally the holes were dug, and Bob turned off the road drill.

"Now, Scoop," he said. "Let's have those edging stones."

Bob lifted the big stones out of Scoop's front shovel and put them down.

"Oh, no. They're too big!" he cried. "We'll have to go back to the yard and get the right ones," he told Scoop.

"No prob, Bob!" Scoop replied cheerfully.

Bob told Dizzy and Muck to wait outside the town hall, just in case the delivery man turned up with the bollards.

"Bye!" called Muck and Dizzy as Bob and Scoop rumbled off.

Back at the yard, Wendy was on the phone to Mrs Potts, who was worried because her statues hadn't been delivered.

"I have to go out to the shops," she flustered.

"Don't worry," soothed Wendy. "I'm sure your statues won't arrive while you're out."

Wendy smiled as she put down the phone. "Dear Mrs Potts. She's always worrying about something!"

Muck and Dizzy were also waiting for a delivery. They were very surprised when a lorry load of garden statues was left on the pavement in front of the town hall. Two dancing fairies, a pixie, a goblin, a windmill and a Greek god!

"Hee, hee, hee! That pixie looks like Lofty in a bad mood!" giggled Dizzy.

Muck laughed at one of the statues that was waving its arms in the air.

"This fairy looks just like Spud scaring away the birds!"

Suddenly Dizzy had one of her great ideas.

"Muck! Why don't we surprise Bob and put the statues up for him?"

"Yeah!" replied an excited Muck.

Dizzy quickly mixed up some concrete and poured it into the holes, then Muck pushed the statues into place with his front shovel.

"Up a bit… to me a bit!" Dizzy directed.

Muck staggered under the weight of the heavy goblin.

"Put it **there!**" cried Dizzy.

"**Pheww!**" Muck sighed with relief as he plonked the statue down.

Dizzy and Muck looked very pleased with themselves as they stared at the statues.

One of the fairies was upside down, the windmill was stuck in sideways, the goblin had gone in head-first and the Greek god had fallen over!

"**Wow!** We're really good at this," said Muck.

Dizzy jumped up and down with excitement.

"Muck!" she squeaked. "Why don't we go and help Mrs Potts next?"

"Yeah," Muck agreed. "It'll be another big surprise for Bob!"

At Mrs Potts' house, they found a pile of bollards neatly stacked by the back door.

"Look, Muck," said Dizzy. "Mrs Potts has left everything out for us."

"What does she want bollards for?" puzzled Muck.

"Maybe she thinks they're pretty!" giggled Dizzy.

"Pretty ugly!" sniggered Muck.

Dizzy carefully poured concrete into the holes that Bob had dug in Mrs Potts' garden. Muck picked up the bollards and dropped them in one by one.
Plop! Plop! Plop!

Meanwhile, Bob and Scoop were outside the town hall, staring in horror at Mrs Potts' statues.

"I don't believe it!" gasped Bob.

"Bob, if the statues are **here**," Scoop spluttered, waving his scoop, "**Where** are the bollards?"

Bob went very pale and put his hands to his head.

"Oh, Scoop," he gulped. "You don't think...?"

Scoop's pistons popped as he asked the big question: "Where are Dizzy and Muck?"

"**Oh, no! Not Mrs Potts' garden!**" yelled Bob.

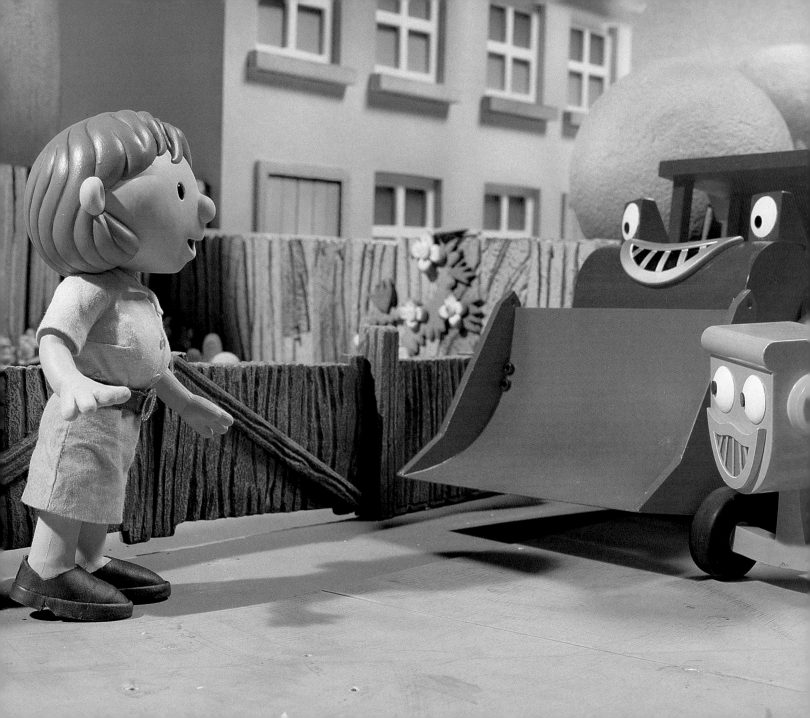

When Mrs Potts came back from the shops and saw the bollards stuck outside her front door, she stared in amazement.

"Where are my garden statues?" gasped Mrs Potts.

"Do you like them?" Dizzy asked proudly.

"What's going on?" Mrs Potts asked.

Dizzy and Muck looked at each other.

"Your statues?" asked Muck.

"Er, well, er, we thought… er…" dithered Dizzy as she realised what they'd done.

Just then, Bob came roaring up, on Scoop.

"What have they done?" Mrs Potts asked.

Bob stared at Dizzy and Muck, and then at Mrs Potts' front garden.

"Oh, dear!" he groaned.

"We were only trying to help!" cried Muck.
"R-e-a-l-l-y we were," Dizzy insisted.
"But… where are my statues?" wondered Mrs Potts.
"Don't worry," Bob assured her. "I know exactly where your statues are."

While Muck and Dizzy moved the bollards to the town hall, Bob, Scoop and Lofty took the statues to Mrs Potts' garden.

"Er... what shall I do with
this, Bob?" asked Lofty, as he
dangled the Greek god from
his hook.

"Put it right here," said Bob,
carefully lowering the statue into
a hole in the garden.

"My Greek god!" cried Mrs Potts in delight. "That's the
one I couldn't remember."

At last, all the statues were safely stuck in their holes.

"Oh! Aren't they beautiful?" Mrs Potts beamed.

"Er... they're very nice," Bob muttered politely.

Mrs Potts picked up her frog statue.

"Oh dear, what about him?" asked Bob.

"He's a little present for you!" laughed Mrs Potts as she pushed the frog into Bob's hands.

Bob stared at the frog and started to laugh. "Thank you, Mrs Potts. He's just what I always wanted!"

THE END!

It was early morning in Bob's Building Yard. Bob was getting ready to go to the pond and put up a new sign.

"Here's your toolbox," whispered Wendy, as she passed him the heavy box. "Why are you whispering?" asked Dizzy.

"Roley and Muck worked late last night," Wendy replied. "So we're giving them a few hours extra sleep."

Bob climbed aboard Scoop. "Let's go," he said leading Lofty and Dizzy out of the yard.

Down the road Spud was complaining to Travis.

"Being a scarecrow isn't as easy as you think," he grumbled.

Suddenly the rickety old gate he was leaning against gave way and Spud fell flat on his back.

"Hee, hee, hee!" giggled Travis.

"Right, that's **it!**" said Spud crossly. "I'm going to get a new job. I could be a pilot!"

"You can't fly!" laughed Travis.

"I could learn," insisted Spud. Spreading his arms like aeroplane wings, he screeched up and down the road.

Bob and the machines came chugging around the corner and almost crashed into Spud.

"Look out!" yelled Bob. Scoop slammed on his brakes sending Bob's toolbox flying.

"Spud! You know you should never play near roads!" cried Bob.

"Sorry, Bob," muttered Spud.

"Could you go and tell Farmer Pickles that I won't be able to fix the window frames in the old cottage until tomorrow?" Bob asked the naughty scarecrow.

"I'm on the job, Bob!" grinned Spud.

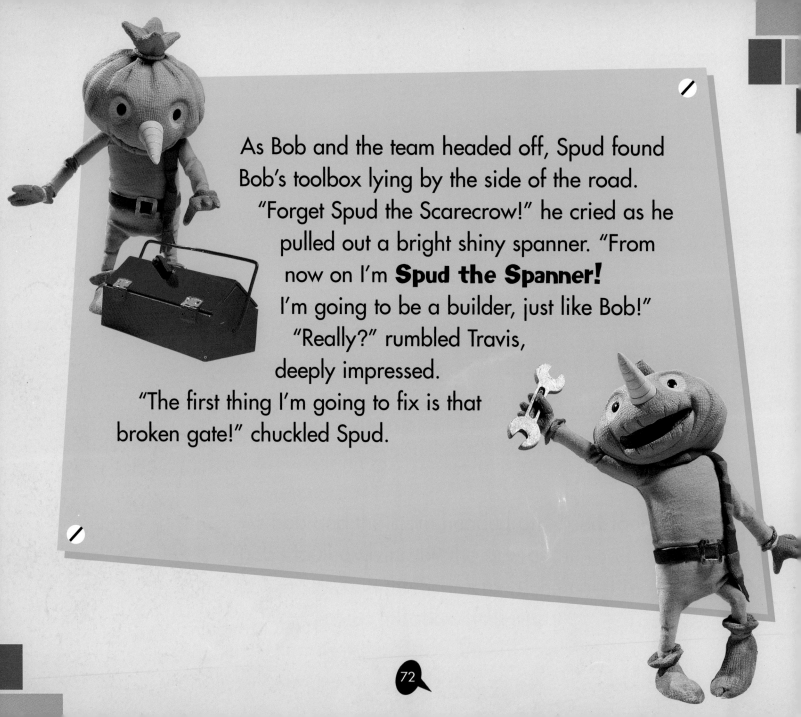

As Bob and the team headed off, Spud found Bob's toolbox lying by the side of the road. "Forget Spud the Scarecrow!" he cried as he pulled out a bright shiny spanner. "From now on I'm **Spud the Spanner!** I'm going to be a builder, just like Bob!"

"Really?" rumbled Travis, deeply impressed.

"The first thing I'm going to fix is that broken gate!" chuckled Spud.

When Bob got to the duck pond he discovered that his toolbox was missing.

"My favourite new spanner's in it," he moaned.

Bob asked Lofty to go back and see if it had fallen out during the journey.

Lofty nervously did a three point turn and rumbled off to look for the missing toolkit.

Meanwhile Spud was mending the gate.
"It looks a bit wobbly," Travis remarked.
"It's meant to look like that!" Spud insisted.
"This building stuff's easy," he continued,
"I think I'll go and fix the cottage windows
next. You can be my machine,
Travis," Spud suggested.
"Oh, no! Not me!" cried Travis.
"Farmer Pickles wants me to plough
a field this afternoon." And with
that Travis drove off.

77

Spud set off down the lane where he found Lofty looking for Bob's toolbox.

"Is this it?" asked Spud, holding up the toolbox he was carrying.

"Er, yes," Lofty said nervously. "C… can I have it, please?"

"Only if you help me with a bit of building first," Spud said.

Lofty didn't really like the idea but he agreed to help.

"**Hurray!**" yelled Spud as he jumped onto Lofty, "I've got a machine! Now I'm a proper builder. Lofty and Spud are on the job!"

At the duck pond Bob waited and waited for Lofty.

"I'd better phone Wendy and get her to send my spare box over," he told Dizzy.

Wendy sent Muck off with the spare toolkit straight away. On his way he bumped into Lofty and Spud.

"Can't stop, Muck," said Spud importantly, "We're busy."

As Spud and Lofty roared past, Muck noticed Bob's other toolbox dangling from Lofty's hook.

"Hey, **STOP!**" he yelled.

Spud and Lofty pulled up outside the old cottage.

"I think I'll start on the front door," beamed Spud.

"Erm… well… are you sure you know what you're doing?" dithered Lofty as he lowered the toolbox to the ground.

"Don't worry! Spud the Builder's on the job!"

"Oh, er…," whimpered Lofty, "I can't look!"

Bob, Scoop and Dizzy were feeding the ducks when Muck came panting up to them.

"Bob! Bob!" he spluttered as he tried to catch his breath. "I've just seen Lofty with Spud. Spud's got your lost toolbox and he's on his way to fix the old cottage!" Muck gasped.

"Let's go team!" cried Bob as he jumped aboard Scoop. "We've got to stop Spud before he hurts himself!"

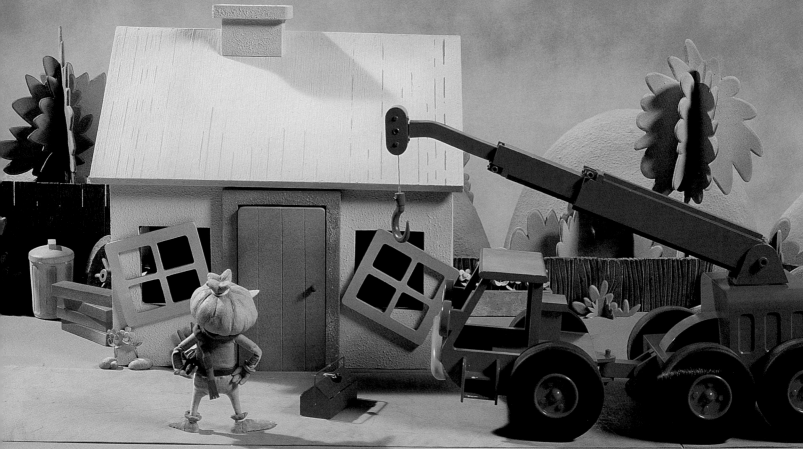

At the old cottage, Spud stepped back to admire his work.

"Not a bad job!" he said proudly.

Lofty clanked nervously. "Er, but… erm… all the windows are crooked!"

"That's how they're supposed to look!" laughed Spud. "Come on, Lofty," he added excitedly, "We've got another job to do. One of the barns has a bit of the roof missing and we're going to fix it!"

Bob arrived with Scoop, Muck and Dizzy. They couldn't believe their eyes when they saw the mess Spud had made of the old cottage.

"Oh, no!" cried Bob. "We'd better sort the windows out before there is an accident. I wonder if there's anything else that needs fixing?" Bob said as he leant back on the door, which collapsed.

"**Ahhh!**" yelled Bob as he fell over backwards.

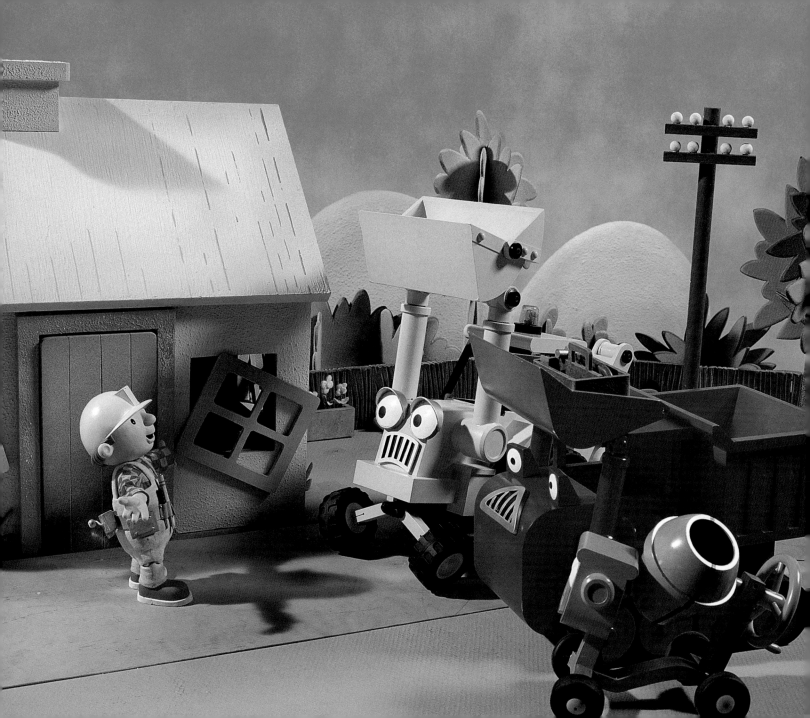

At the barn Spud strapped a sheet of roofing onto his back, and got Lofty to lift him onto the roof.

"This is exciting," he said, "I've never fixed a roof before."

"Be careful, Spud!" pleaded Lofty.

"Don't you worry," laughed Spud. "This is a job for Spud the Spanner!"

Just then a huge gust of wind blew him off the roof!

Spud sailed through the air like a bird, high above Lofty's head.

"**H-E-L-P!**" cried Spud as the wind blew him on.

Back at the cottage, Muck looked up at the sky. "What's that?" he wondered.

"**Wow!**" Dizzy squeaked excitedly. "It looks like a flying Spud!"

They all stared up at Spud who was flying straight towards them.

"**Whey! Arrrghh!**" Spud bawled as he landed on the chimney of the old cottage.

"Nice landing, Spud," chuckled Bob.

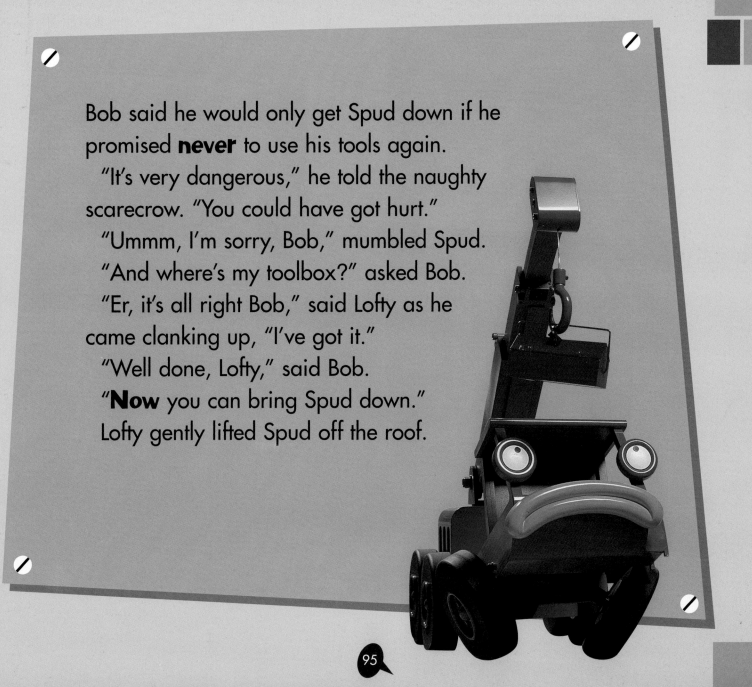

Bob said he would only get Spud down if he promised **never** to use his tools again.

"It's very dangerous," he told the naughty scarecrow. "You could have got hurt."

"Ummm, I'm sorry, Bob," mumbled Spud.

"And where's my toolbox?" asked Bob.

"Er, it's all right Bob," said Lofty as he came clanking up, "I've got it."

"Well done, Lofty," said Bob.

"**Now** you can bring Spud down."

Lofty gently lifted Spud off the roof.

"I think I'll stay a scarecrow," Spud announced. "It's much safer than being a builder!"

THE END!

Mucky Muck

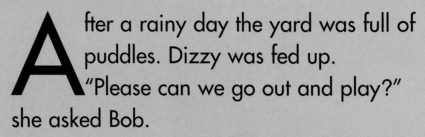

After a rainy day the yard was full of puddles. Dizzy was fed up.

"Please can we go out and play?" she asked Bob.

"No, Dizzy," he said. "You'll get dirty, just like Scoop and Muck."

"But it's lovely being dirty!" cried Muck.

Wendy was at the farm, repairing the guttering on Farmer Pickles's roof.

"How's it going?" Farmer Pickles shouted up to her.

"It doesn't look good," Wendy replied. "You haven't just got a broken gutter, there's a crack in the drainpipe too.
Lofty and I have got quite a bit of work to do."

Back at the yard, Bob put on his apron and filled up a bucket with warm, soapy water.

"Who's first for a wash?" he asked.

"Ooh, me please!" giggled Dizzy.

"You're not even dirty!" laughed Bob. "I'll start with Scoop."

Muck huddled up close to Roley. "I'm glad I'm not first. I don't want to be washed. I love being mucky."

"That's why you're called Muck!" chuckled Roley.

Bob covered Scoop in soapy bubbles, then connected the hose pipe to the tap, so that he could rinse him clean. He didn't realise that his foot was on the hose pipe, blocking off the water.

"What's going on?" wondered Bob as he peered down the empty nozzle. Suddenly he lifted up his foot and the water swooshed out, all over his face and all over the yard.

"Oohh, noooo!" spluttered Bob.

104

Meanwhile, Spud had been sheltering from the rain in Travis's trailer.

When he saw it had stopped, he threw back the waterproof cover he'd been lying under and jumped out.

"Thanks, Travis," he said. "I hate getting wet."

"That's all right," said Travis and revved up his engine to move forward. His wheels span around, but Travis didn't move. He was stuck tight in the deep mud.

"I'll never get out!" he wailed.

"Hang on," said Spud. "I'll go and get Farmer Pickles."

Back at the yard, Bob had just finished giving Scoop a wash down. His yellow paintwork gleamed brightly.
"Right, now it's your turn, Muck," said Bob.
"Can Roley go before me?" he begged.
"You're not frightened of a drop of water, are you?" laughed Bob.
"No, of course not," said Muck, very nervously.

108

Just then, Bob's mobile phone started ringing.

"Hang on, Muck," he said. When he'd finished his call, Bob turned to the machines, "That was Farmer Pickles. Travis is stuck in the mud," he said.

"I can pull him out!" cried Scoop.

"Your wheels might get stuck too," said Bob. "I think I'll use Muck. His caterpillar treads are built for this kind of job."

"That's lucky," Muck whispered to Roley. "Now I can stay mucky!"

"Bob, please can I come too?" asked Dizzy.

"All right," said Bob.

"Hurray!" squeaked Dizzy.

"**Can we help him?**" Bob called out.

"**Yes, we can!**" the machines shouted back.

Bob, Muck and Dizzy set off for the farm.

"Emergency! Woo! Woo!" squeaked Dizzy, pretending to have a siren like a police car.

When they arrived at the field, they could see that Travis was well and truly stuck.

"Don't worry, Travis," called Bob. "We'll have you out in no time."

Bob tied one end of a rope around Travis's axle and the other end to Muck's tow bar. "Can you tow it, Muck?" he called.

"**YES**... hummpf!" spluttered Muck as he struggled to turn his big caterpillar wheels. "**I**... Ufff! **CAN!**" said Muck tugging hard.

Suddenly Travis's wheels started to spin and then they both shot forwards, sending a shower of mud everywhere!

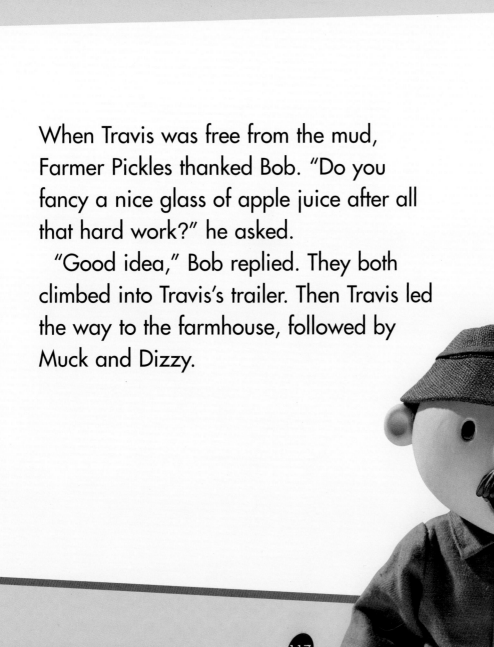

When Travis was free from the mud, Farmer Pickles thanked Bob. "Do you fancy a nice glass of apple juice after all that hard work?" he asked.

"Good idea," Bob replied. They both climbed into Travis's trailer. Then Travis led the way to the farmhouse, followed by Muck and Dizzy.

As they trundled along the lane Spud popped up, holding a big, sloppy mud pie.

"Hey, Dizzy, over here!" he called. Dizzy turned around and Spud threw the mud pie straight into her face. Splat! Mud trickled down Dizzy's nose making her giggle.

"Oooh, it's all squishy!" she squealed. Spud threw an even bigger mud pie at Muck.

"A mud pie fight!" yelled Muck. In their excitement, Dizzy and Muck forgot all about keeping up with Travis and Bob.

When Bob arrived at the farmhouse he found Lofty
and Wendy fitting the last section of guttering.

"How are you getting on?" he called up to her.

"Fine," Wendy replied. "So you managed
to pull Travis out of the mud?"

"Yes. Muck did well, didn't you?"
Bob said as he turned around to
talk to Muck. But the digger
machine wasn't there. "Where
have Muck and Dizzy gone?"
he gasped.

Muck was still having a wonderful time in the field.

"If I was as little as you, Dizzy, I'd roll over and wriggle in this lovely, squishy mud!" he said.

"**Wheee!**" squeaked Dizzy as she flipped onto her back and rolled in the mud like a little puppy.

Suddenly they heard Bob's voice. "Dizzy! Muck! What's going on?" he shouted.

"Er, we were just having a game of mud pies," muttered Muck.

"We were worried. You had all better get back to the farm, right now," said Bob. "Farmer Pickles has got a surprise for you."

Back at the farm, Bob lined up Muck, Dizzy and Spud, and told them to close their eyes.

"Ooh, I hope it's something really scrummy!" said Spud hungrily.

"Ready?" Bob asked, as Wendy and Farmer Pickles came out of the house with buckets of soapy water.

"Ready!" laughed Wendy.

Wendy dipped her brush into the water and started to wash the mud off Dizzy's mixer.

"Ooh, ooh, that tickles!" Dizzy giggled. Muck wanted to open his eyes when he heard Dizzy laugh.

"No peeping, Muck!" called Wendy.

But when it came to Muck's turn he got a nasty shock.

"Arghh!" he yelled as Wendy splashed water all over him.

"Now it's your turn, Spud," said Farmer Pickles.

"Oh, no!" cried Spud. He turned to run away, but skidded in a muddy puddle.

"Owww!" Spud cried, as he fell flat on his face and bent his nose. "Has anyone got a new parsnip?"

THE END!